ROCK☆A☆BYE
FARM

ROCK★A★BYE
FARM

by Diane Johnston Hamm

illustrated by Rick Brown

HALF MOON BOOKS
Published by Simon & Schuster
New York   London   Toronto   Sydney   Tokyo   Singapore

HALF MOON BOOKS
An imprint of Simon & Schuster
1230 Avenue of the Americas, New York, New York 10020
Text copyright © 1992 by Diane Johnston Hamm
Illustrations copyright © 1992 by Richard Brown
Also available in a SIMON & SCHUSTER
BOOKS FOR YOUNG READERS hardcover edition.
Designed by Lucille Chomowicz
The text of this book is set in Breughel 55.
The illustrations were done in ink and watercolor.
Manufactured in the United States
10 9 8 7 6 5 4 3 2 1
Library of Congress Cataloging-in-Publication Data
Hamm, Diane Johnston. Rockabye farm/by Diane Hamm: illustrated by
Richard Brown. Summary: The Farmer helps his family and barnyard
animals fall asleep before drifting off himself. [1. Sleep —Fiction.]
I. Brown, Richard, 1941-   ill. II. Title.PZ7.H1837R63   1992
[E] — dc20 91-19127
ISBN 0-671-74773-8   ISBN 0-671-88630-4 (pbk)

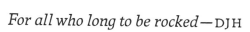 *For all who long to be rocked*—DJH

 *To William Ross IV*—RB

ROCK·A·BYE FARM

It is bedtime.

The Farmer rocks his baby.

When the baby goes to sleep,

the Farmer rocks his dog.

When the dog is snoring loudly,

the Farmer rocks his hen.

When the hen has settled down,

the Farmer rocks his sheep.

When the sheep are dreaming well,

the Farmer rocks his pig.

When the pig no longer squeals,

the Farmer rocks his cow.

When the cow is tucked in straw,

the Farmer rocks his horse.

When the horse's eyelids close,

the Farmer rocks the mouse.

Now that everyone's asleep...

the Farmer rocks himself.

Good-Night.